For Gia, my very first niece.
You taught me everything there is to know
about city kids—and I love you so.
—E.O.

To Mom and Dad for having given me the chance
of growing as a person, in new lands.
—A.L.

I Can Read® and I Can Read Book® are trademarks of HarperCollins Publishers.

Reina Ramos Works It Out
Text copyright © 2022 by Emma Otheguy
Illustrations copyright © by Andrés Landazábal
All rights reserved. Printed in the United States of America.
No part of this book may be used or reproduced in any manner whatsoever without written permission except
in the case of brief quotations embodied in critical articles and reviews. For information address
HarperCollins Children's Books, a division of HarperCollins Publishers,
195 Broadway, New York, NY 10007.
www.icanread.com

Library of Congress Control Number: 2022938055
ISBN 978-0-06-322311-0 (trade bdg.) — ISBN 978-0-06-322310-3 (pbk.)

Book design by Elaine Lopez-Levine

22 23 24 25 26 LB 10 9 8 7 6 5 4 3 2 1 ❖ First Edition

Reina Ramos

Works It Out!

by Emma Otheguy

pictures by Andrés Landazábal

HARPER

An Imprint of HarperCollins Publishers

Mr. Li has big news.

Our class will be a wax museum!

We will dress up as famous stars

and stand like wax statues.

When our families visit,
we will come to life!

I know!

I will be Frida Kahlo.

She was a strong person like

my mami and abuela—and me!

Frida wore flowers in her hair.

I have the perfect headband.

I will glue flowers to it.

At recess, I run to Nora.

"Do you know about Frida Kahlo?"
I ask Nora.

"I LOVE Frida," Nora says.
"She was a painter—just like me!"
We dance around the playground
shouting, "FRIDA! FRIDA!"

After school, I work on my costume.

"Nora might want to be Frida,"
Abuela tells me.

"She loves art."

But I am busy gluing flowers.

Then Abuela turns on Celia Cruz,

the famous salsa star

who liked to say "¡Azúcar!"

That means sugar!

I dance and sing along.

"¡Azúcar!"

The next day, we pick our parts.

Carlos will be Roberto Clemente.

Lila will be Ellen Ochoa.

Then Nora picks—Frida Kahlo!

How could she do this to me?

Nora tries to get my attention.

I turn away.

At lunch, I stay inside.

I grab paints from the art corner.

I'll make a beautiful painting

to prove that I am the BEST Frida!

Oh NO! I spilled!

My painting is an ugly mush,

and there is paint everywhere.

Nora opens the door.

"Why aren't you at lunch, Reina?"

"You took Frida from me!" I say.

"I didn't know you wanted Frida!"

"You didn't?" I whisper.

"I thought you were giving me her

because I like painting.

But now you're ruining it!" Nora says.

"I'm sorry, Nora," I say.

"I thought you were being mean."

Mr. Li walks in.

Uh-oh. I think I'm in trouble.

Spilled paint is still everywhere.

"What happened?" Mr. Li asks.

I burst into tears.

When Nora sees me crying,
she picks up a sponge.
"Don't worry, Reina!"

Nora helps me clean up.

Then she turns my mush painting

into beautiful flowers.

Nora and I share a big hug.

"Nora should be Frida,"

I tell Mr. Li.

"She is a great artist and a great friend.

And I have the perfect headband

for her costume!"

After school,

I tell Abuela the whole story.

"I am glad I made up with Nora.

But now I have no one to be.

I wanted to be a strong person!"

"You are strong," Abuela says.

"You gave up Frida for your friend."

"¡Ven!" Abuela dances to Celia Cruz.

Suddenly I have a GREAT idea!

My name is Reina—that means queen.

28

I love to dance, and dancers
are strong.
I will be Celia Cruz,
Queen of Salsa!

The day of the wax museum,

Nora and I stand very still.

She wears my flower headband.

I wear sequins and sparkles.

When families visit,

I come to life and dance.

"¡Azúcar!"

Spanish words in this book:

Abuela: Grandma

¡Azúcar!: Sugar! Celia Cruz liked
to say this when she sang.

Reina: Queen, and also a common girl's name

¡Ven!: Come on!

Famous people in this book:

Roberto Clemente:
A Puerto Rican
baseball player

Celia Cruz:
A Cuban
singer

Frida Kahlo:
A Mexican
painter

Ellen Ochoa:
A Latina
astronaut